Ma Jiang
and the
Orange Ants

BY BARBARA ANN PORTE

ILLUSTRATED BY ANNIE CANNON

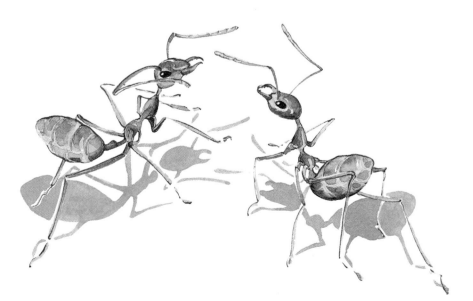

ORCHARD BOOKS · NEW YORK

To my friends in Oak Ridge, Tennessee,
who tell me things I need to know to write
my books—especially Donna and Dave
Reichle, Mimi and Murray Rosenthal,
Sheila and Mike Saltmarsh, Nancy and
Bob Van Hook.—B.A.P.

To Barbara Ann and to Anne B. for their
care in detecting the future in the past
and the past in the future.—A.C.

AGES AGO IN CHINA a little girl named Ma Jiang lived with her mother and her father and her three brothers. Two of the brothers were nearly grown, but the third one, Bao, was still a baby. Selling orange ants was how the Ma family earned their living. Though it didn't make them rich, they had everything they needed to get by: food, clothes, shelter, and medicine to put on ant bites.

Orange ants are very fierce. They eat almost every crawling thing in sight, and whatever gets in their way, they bite. They especially like to dine on insects that eat oranges, which is how they got their name. Orange growers in China buy orange ants and put them in their orange groves to protect the fruit from harm.

Long ago some of the ants bought by orange growers
had been caught by the Ma family.
Night after night Jiang's father and her brothers climbed
high into tall trees and into wild bamboo, where orange
ants live, and cut down their nests while the ants were
asleep. Then, wrapping the nests securely in
woven rush-mat bags, they
carried them back to
Jiang's mother.

She took the ants, still in their nests, inside the bags, to market to sell.

Jiang had her own job to do. She helped look after the baby. "Surely in all of China there has never been a better baby," she sometimes said.

The family probably would have gone on this way too—but one terrible day soldiers descended from the north, rounding up all eligible men to serve in the emperor's army. Among those rounded up were Jiang's father and her older brothers. How dreadful! Where would they be taken? No one knew. What would they be made to do when they got there? No one knew that either. And worst of all—no one knew when, if ever, they would be allowed to return. Tears filled all the Mas' eyes as they said their good-byes.

Who will look after this family now, Jiang worried. So did her mother. Selling orange ants was one thing—catching them was another. Who would climb the trees?

Jiang's mother didn't know how. "Waste of time, that tree climbing. Attend to your weaving," her parents had told her when she was growing up. So she was very good at making rush-mat bags and also baskets and other woven articles. As for Jiang, she was too small to climb so high and too young to be out alone after dark.

Thank goodness! she thought. Though brave in other ways, Jiang did not care to get too near wild nests of orange ants. "Killer ants," she told the baby. "They think whatever moves is food, including fingers and toes."

"Tuh-oh," Bao said, as though in agreement. Or perhaps hoping to be fed.

By now the last of the captured orange ants had been sold, and money was scarce. Meals were further apart than they'd been in the past, and portions much smaller. Sometimes Bao was hungry, and so was Jiang. Their mother was too, but what could she do? She was doing her best.

Every minute she could she spent weaving rush-mat bags; and also baskets, trays, sieves, chicken cages, sandals, floor mats, fans, fish traps, and nets to sell in the market. But only the very rich or the very lazy bought them. Others wove their own.

As the family grew poorer and poorer, Jiang's mother worked harder and longer. More and more of the baby's daily care was left to Jiang. How she longed for her father and her brothers to come home.

"If only I were taller and less afraid of bites, we might have more to eat," Jiang told the hungry baby.

"Eek," Bao said sadly, and sucked his thumb.

Then one day their mother had a bit of good luck. As she sat at market tending her wares, an old man approached her. He trapped bees and sold their honey for a living.

"Why, this is just what I need for staving off stings," he told her, draping himself in rush-mat nets, plopping a chicken cage over his head, and trying on sandals. Short of money, he offered to pay in honey.

"Why not?" Jiang's mother said. "Honey makes everything taste better." Carrying the honey home in a gourd, she hung it from a ceiling hook for safekeeping.

That night, after a meager dinner of bean and rice gruel, she took down the honey, dipped a pair of chopsticks into it, and gave Jiang and the baby each a lick. "You can have more tomorrow if you're good," she promised, hanging the honey back up.

"Goo," said Bao, and licked his lips.

The following day, while their mother was away gathering rushes to weave, Jiang took her brother outside. She sat him on the ground beside a pile of rocks. "Blocks," she told him. He played for a while, but then got bored and began to fuss.

"Are you hungry? Do you want something to eat?" Jiang asked.

"Eat," Bao said, and stuck out his tongue.

Surprised to hear him speak so clearly, Jiang went inside, climbed onto a stool, and got the honey. She carried it back, along with a pair of chopsticks.

"Have some," she said, dipping a stick into the honey, then holding it out. Bao licked the stick, then smacked his lips.

"More?" asked Jiang.

"More," said Bao. "More, more, more." So for the next little while, Jiang was kept busy dipping chopsticks into honey, taking turns with her brother licking it off. The honey was sweet and very good. It was also rather messy and hard to keep from dripping.

"Enough?" Jiang finally asked. Too sticky to speak, Bao burped and bobbed his head. "Well, the same to you," said Jiang. Then she carried the honey and the chopsticks back inside, rehung the gourd from the ceiling hook, and put back the stool.

When she returned, she saw that her brother was staring at something moving on the ground. Looking down, Jiang saw it was a small puddle of honey, crawling with ants—hundreds of ants and hundreds more on the way. "Aiyee," she screeched and snatched up Bao.

"Bwaa, bwaa," the startled baby complained.

"Hush," Jiang soothed. "Black ants won't bite."

"Bite," Bao said, and struggled to get down.

"Nap time," Jiang told him. Carrying him indoors, she laid him in bed.

"No nap," said Bao, but in almost no time he was snoring. While he slept, Jiang had time to think.

Of course, of course—a honey trap. What could be simpler? she asked herself. Or safer? Was there ever an ant, whatever its color, that didn't like honey? Why hadn't she thought of it before? Jiang looked around the room for something to use. Seeing one of her mother's tightly woven rush-mat bags, she picked it up, unfastened it at the top, and smeared the inside with honey.

Retying the bag carefully, she left a small opening. Finally, making sure that Bao was sound asleep, she slipped outside to hang her homemade trap on a low bamboo branch.

The next day when she went to check, the rush-mat bag was filled with orange ants. Cautiously, Jiang closed up the bag, took it down, and carried it home to show her mother.

"Ai-yo," her mother said happily. "It looks as if we're back in the orange ant business."

To show how pleased she was with Jiang, she gave her a double helping of rice for dinner with honey on the side.

"Thank you," said Jiang. "But you know, if not for Bao's wanting a snack, I never would have thought of it." And she shared her extra portion with him.

"Thank you," said Bao. Imagine how surprised his mother was to hear him speak!

Later that same night, Jiang and her mother smeared honey inside a dozen rush-mat bags. In the morning, Jiang hung them in trees where orange ants nested. Every day she checked on them and, as they filled with orange ants, collected the bags and carried them home to her mother, who took them to market and sold them.

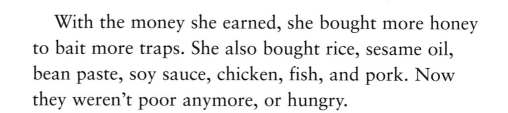

With the money she earned, she bought more honey to bait more traps. She also bought rice, sesame oil, bean paste, soy sauce, chicken, fish, and pork. Now they weren't poor anymore, or hungry.

This made them happier than they'd been for some time, but not completely. How could they be—a family of six, after all, but only three of them at home.

Time came, time went. Spring turned to summer and summer to fall. Winter set in. The New Year was coming. Throughout the village everyone was getting ready for the celebration: grinding wheat; cooking and cleaning; covering walls, windows, and doors with decorations. Jiang and her mother were getting ready too.

"At least we'll have plenty to eat," Jiang's mother said to herself as she sliced meat and vegetables, stuffed dumplings, rolled noodles, steamed cakes, and did a hundred and one other things to prepare for the festival. As she worked, a tear rolled down her cheek. If only her husband and her sons could be with them to share in the feast, she thought.

"At least we have lots of fine pictures," Jiang told herself, as she pasted one of a fierce-looking tiger onto the door. Then stepping back to see it better, she frowned. If only her father and her brothers could be with them to welcome in the New Year.

At that moment Bao toddled by. Seeing the tiger, he stopped in his tracks. "Grrr! Grrr!" he roared at it. He showed play claws and giggled. Probably he's too young to remember our father or our brothers, Jiang thought. How sad!

Then, just three days before the end of the old year, when snow was on the ground, there came a tramping sound. "Soldiers," said the villagers, and rushed off to hide in their houses. Jiang and her mother were already in their house, salting fish in the kitchen. Bao was banging a pot. They paused to peek out. What a frightening sight! A grisly looking group of weirdly dressed men were climbing the hill, packs on their backs, their bodies bundled against the cold.

Bandits, decided Jiang's mother, and shivered. As she backed away from the window, several of the bandits broke free of the rest and ran straight for the Ma family's front door. They banged with no sign of stopping when they got there. Afraid they'd break down the door, Jiang's mother pushed Jiang and the baby behind her and opened it a crack.

Fearfully she watched as the bandits pulled back their hats and their face wraps. That's when Jiang's mother could see it was her husband and her two sons, standing there in the doorway, released at last from service to the emperor. Imagine that family's rejoicing! Jiang and her mother and her father and her brothers could hardly stop bowing.

Only Bao sat by himself on the floor, looking around at so much commotion. How he hated being left out. Suddenly he pulled himself to his feet.

"Da da da da," he shrieked, and flung himself at his father.

His father stepped back in surprise. Then, having regained his composure, he reached down and picked up Bao.

"I see while we've been gone, our baby's learned how to speak," he said.

While Jiang's father and her older brothers washed up and changed clothes, Jiang and her mother set out a feast. When everyone had eaten, they exchanged news of all that had happened during their long separation:

"Walls—day after day we spent building walls," Jiang's father said.

"To keep back the northern enemy," explained Jiang's eldest brother.

"The worst part was always being cold," the younger one told them.

Finally it was Jiang's mother's turn. "At first we had problems too," she said. "If not for Jiang, I don't know how we would have managed." Then, holding up an orange ant trap for their inspection, she brought her husband and her sons up-to-date on the family business. Jiang's father and her brothers looked at Jiang approvingly.

"Don't forget the baby," said Jiang. "If he had been a neater eater, I never would have thought of it."

"Eater neater," said Bao, and stuck a fistful of sticky rice in his hair.

So it was that when the New Year arrived, Jiang and her family had everything to be grateful for: good health, a prosperous business, plenty to eat, and everyone together to share it besides. They lived happily for a long time to come.

As for the orange ants, word spread and soon others also began using traps. Eventually hog and sheep bladders replaced the rush-mat bags. Lard was used for bait instead of honey. But the principle remained, and to this day, orange ants still guard the orange groves in parts of China. It has been that way for almost two thousand years.

A NOTE FOR THE READER

The use of carnivorous citrus ants (*Oecophylla smaragdina*) to protect orange groves in China dates back at least 1,700 years. The earliest known mention of such use is attributed to Ji Han in his records of the *Plants and Trees of the Southern Regions* (A.D. 304):

The people of Jiao-zhi sell in their markets ants in bags of rush matting. The nests are like silk. The bags are all attached to twigs and leaves which, with the ants inside the nests, are for sale. The ants are reddish-yellow in color, bigger than ordinary ants. (These ants do not eat the oranges, but attack and kill the insects which do.)

Later, innovations were made in collecting the ants, as described by Zhuang Jiyu in his *Miscellaneous Random Notes* (A.D. 1130):

Fruit-growing families buy these ants from vendors who make a business of collecting and selling such creatures. They trap them by filling hogs' or sheep's bladders with fat and placing them with the cavities open next to the ants' nests. They wait until the ants have migrated into the bladders and then take them away. This is known as *yang kan i*, rearing orange ants.

Over the centuries improvements continued to be made in citrus ant cultivation. At least since 1600, according to a contemporaneous report, bamboo strips were being used to connect trees in orange orchards. Serving as bridges, the strips permitted the ants to travel all over the groves. More recently, starting in the late 1970s, grove owners have begun providing sugar water and fried chicken eggs to help the ants through the winter.

While no word exists as to who first came up with the idea of rearing orange ants (also known in Chinese as *Huang Jin Yi*, yellow fear ant), nor, so far as I know, have rush-mat bags ever been baited with honey, I've no reason to think it couldn't have happened as described in my story. Readers interested in more complete information should consult "The Ancient Cultured Citrus Ant" by H. T. Huang and Pei Yang in *Bioscience,* Volume 37, No. 9 (October 1987), pp. 665–671; and Huang, Hsing-Tsung, "Biological Pest Control," Volume 6, Part 1 (1986), pp. 519–553, in Joseph Needham, *Science and Civilisation in China* (Cambridge, England: Cambridge University Press, 1954–). Readers who want to know more about the weaver class of ant to which the citrus ant belongs should consult *Journey to the Ants: A Story of Scientific Exploration* by Bert Hölldobler and Edward O. Wilson (Cambridge, Mass.: Harvard University Press, 1994).

B.A.P.

Orchard Books, A Grolier Company, 95 Madison Avenue, New York, NY 10016

Manufactured in the United States of America. Printed and bound by Phoenix Color Corp. Book design by Mina Greenstein. Calligraphy by Jeanyee Wong. The text of this book is set in 14 point Sabon. The illustrations are rendered in watercolor, gouache, and ink.
10 9 8 7 6 5 4 3 2 1

Library of Congress Cataloging-in-Publication Data
Porte, Barbara Ann.
Ma Jiang and the orange ants / by Barbara Ann Porte ; illustrated by Annie Cannon.   p.   cm.
Summary: When her father and brother are called away to war, Ma Jiang finds a unique way to trap the orange ants that her mother sells in order to make a living.
ISBN 0-531-30241-5 (trade : alk. paper)—ISBN 0-531-33241-1 (library bdg. : alk. paper)
[1. China—Fiction. 2. Ants—Fiction.] I. Cannon, Annie, ill. II. Title.
PZ7.P7995 Maj 2000 [E]—dc21 99-30234